we walk in sandy places

we walk in sandy places

by BYRD BAYLOR   photographs by MARILYN SCHWEITZER

Charles Scribner's Sons / New York

Text Copyright © 1976 Byrd Baylor
Photographs Copyright © 1976 Marilyn Schweitzer

Library of Congress Cataloging in Publication Data

Baylor, Byrd.
We walk in sandy places.

SUMMARY: When animals cross the desert their tracks
leave behind a story in the sand.
[1. Animals tracks—Fiction. 2. Deserts—Fiction]
I. Schweitzer, Marilyn. II. Title.
PZ7.B3435We   [Fic]   75-8341
ISBN 0-684-14526-X

1 3 5 7 9 11 13 15 17 19   RD/C   20 18 16 14 12 10 8 6 4 2

Printed in the United States of America

To Kit
from Marilyn and Byrd

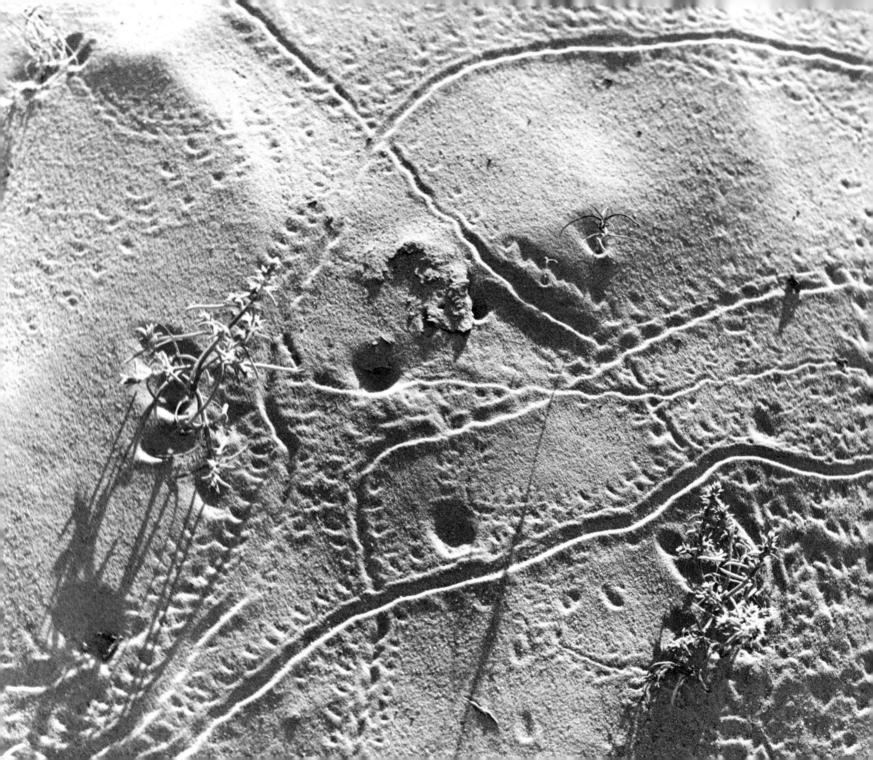

Forgive me for walking here,
Brother Lizard.

Forgive me,
Sister Quail.

I know this is your sand,
not mine.
You've left your tracks
to make it yours.
You've left a hundred
tiny roads.

Spiders
and snakes
and beetles and mice,
don't worry.

You can see that
I walk
lightly
here.

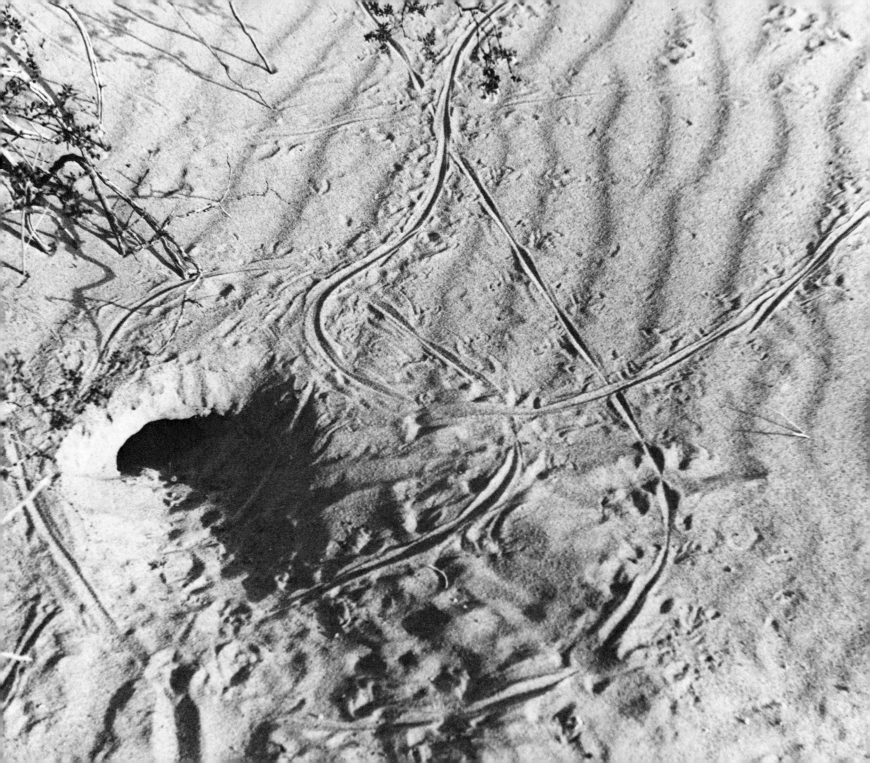

I never ruin
the paths
you've made.
I only follow them
because
they are good paths
to follow.

They're maps
that show
where
small feet
crossed the desert
all last night
and where those feet
circled
and stopped
or where they turned
and chose a hill
or met a friend
or went alone....

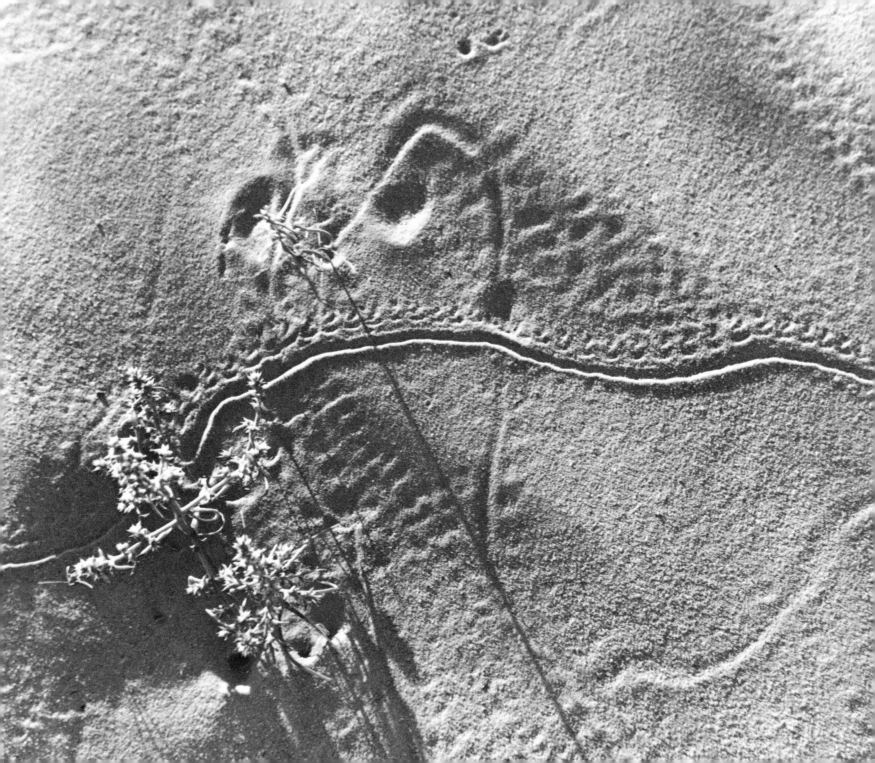

Some people read tracks
like they'd read a story.
(The story is
true.
It's written
in sand.)

Tracks tell
if a mouse
ran fast or slow
and if it carried
something
as it went along.
They tell if it
suddenly
stopped
in fear
and then jumped back
behind a weed
and hid,
quiet
as any stone.

Tracks tell
everything
that happens.
They name
everyone
who passes.

They say that here
a quail
walked in a circle
just to be walking
around in a circle.
Quail
feel that way
sometimes.

And a grasshopper
sailed
through the air
in one giant
green
whistling leap
and plopped down
hard
into the sand.

You see
his landing place.

Sometime last night
a porcupine
crept by.
It moved
with the shadows
at dawn.
Its long quills
brushed the sand.
With every step
it left
another picture.

And a beetle left
his double track
behind him.
He'd walked
across his world
and his world was all
made of sand.
It must have seemed
like forever
to a thing so small.

He's not there yet
(wherever he's going)
but at least he knows
where he wants to be.

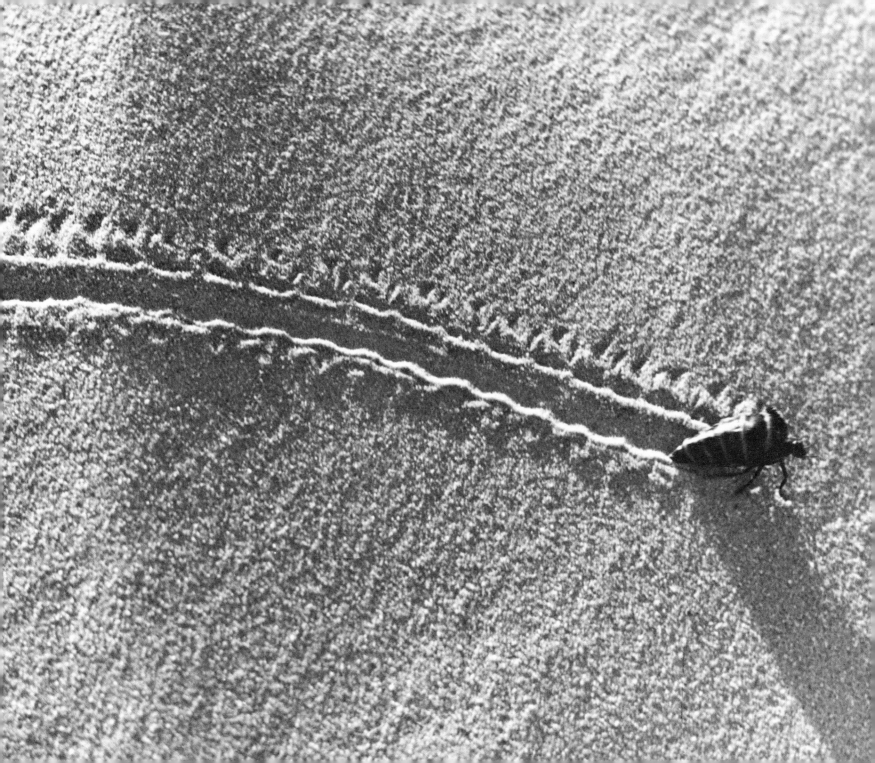

These tracks
say
horned toad
went searching
for his favorite meal
again.
It's a meal
he finds
at ant hills—
when he's lucky.

Here
a skunk
went his own way.
He may still
be somewhere
near.

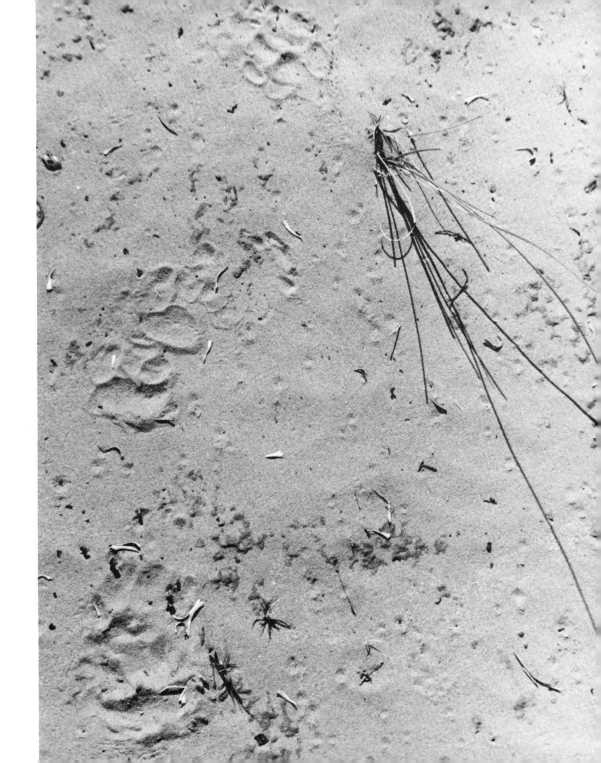

Did something move?
It seemed to be
a soft grey shadow passing...
no more than that.
It seemed to be
only
wind in the weeds,
but
sand holds
this deer track now.

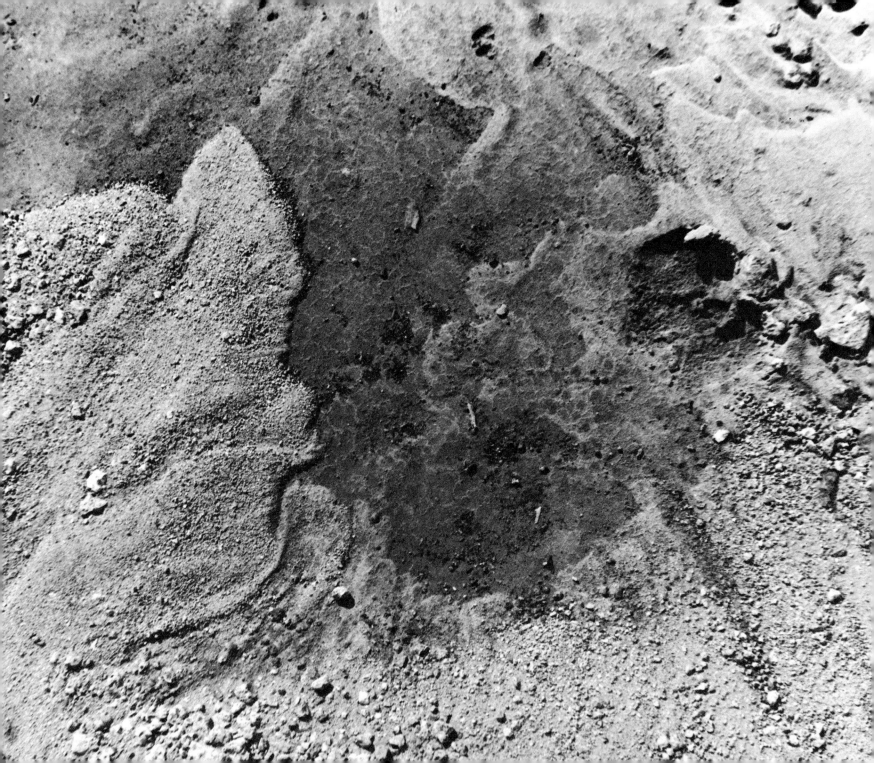

Javelina
came
to the wash
sniffing
for water.

Something
hopped along
and then sat down
lazily
to rest
and hopped again
and sat again
to think
things
over.

It's squirrel.
She's having
breakfast
now.

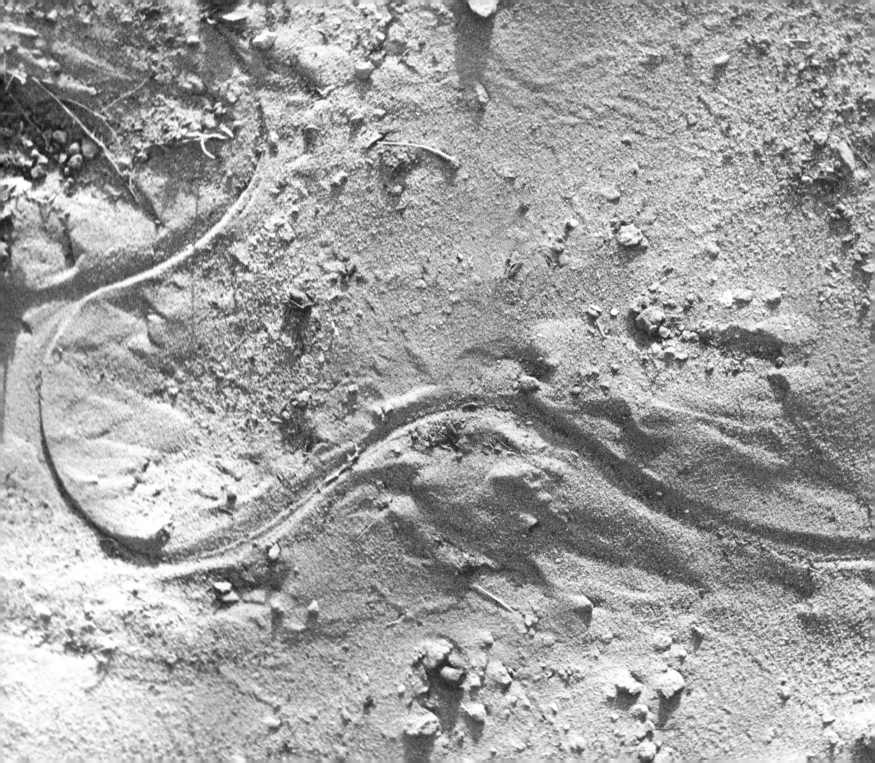

It takes
a long
dragging
lizard tail
to make a track
like this.
And it takes
a lizard
who moves
easy
as wind
and likes
the way he runs
and likes
the feel of sand
on his tail
and on his
long
thin
delicate toes.

These
wide, solid footprints
say
desert tortoise
is taking
an afternoon walk.
She knows
that the earth feels good
after rain,
good for a tortoise
to touch
and to smell.

Bird tracks
are everywhere...
little pointed tracks
that hop along
so lightly
the earth
can hardly feel them.

Here roadrunner
was in a hurry.
Did he see a lizard
over there?

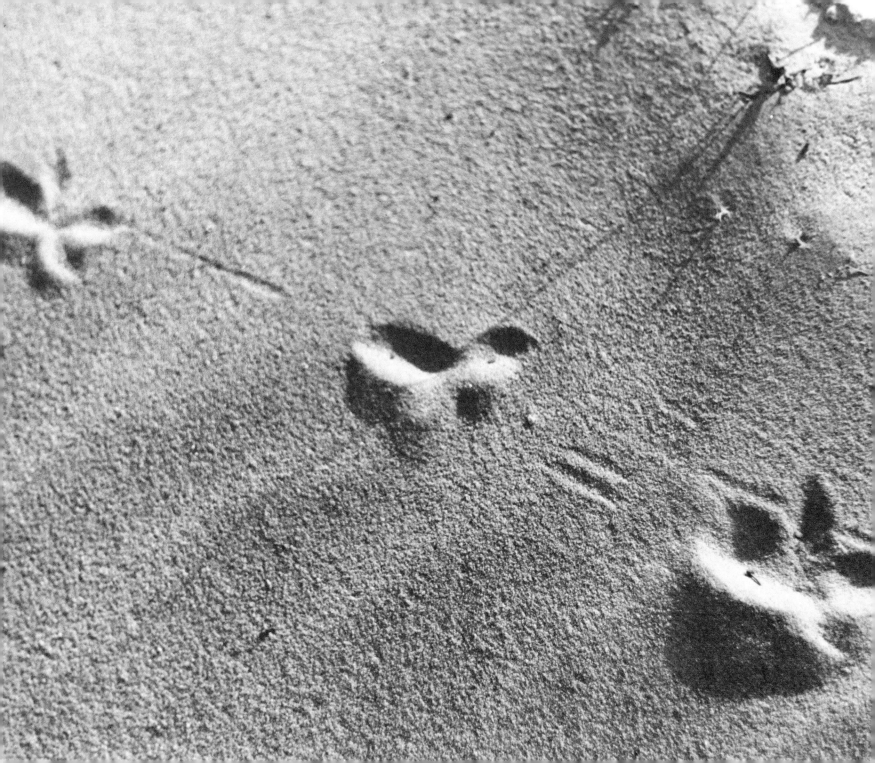

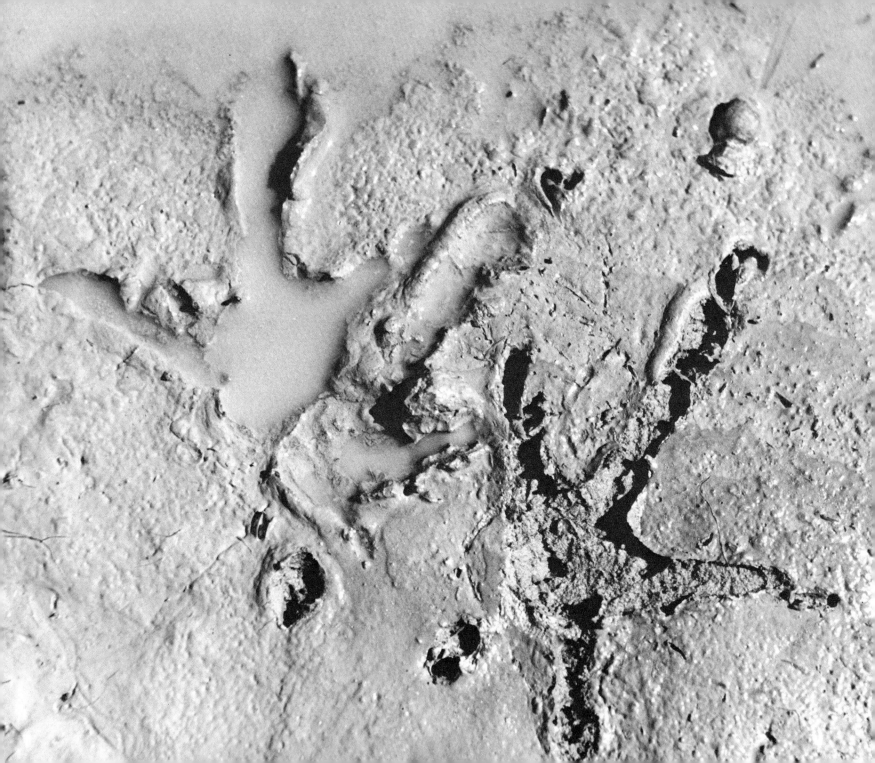

A raven
came down
for a minute
to step
in a cool muddy puddle
left from the rain.
Did he rise again
at once,
dark and restless,
calling out?

Did coyotes
dance
in the moonlight
here?
Did they sing
to one another
as they ran
across the hills?
Did baby rabbits
play
a game of
roll-around
in this soft sand?

All tracks don't wander.
Some lead home.
Tracks come
from all directions...
going home.

A lizard's home?
A squirrel's?
A mouse's?
Whose?

Somebody's
safe
dark
burrow,
somebody's
sandy
underground nest.

Some holes
have flowers
at the door.
Some hide in shade.
Some face the sun.
They all
have paths
that look like
going home.

Today
I want
to make
a path here
too.

Brother Lizard,
I want my path to be
as beautiful
as yours.

Sister Quail,
please show me how
you touch
the sand.

Horned toads,
teach me.
Spiders,
teach me
your way.

Snakes,
I'll learn
from you.

I want
ants
to like
my path.

I want
coyote
to sniff
and know
I am a friend.

I want my path
to look
so natural here
that
rocks
will call to me
the way they call
to lizards

and hills
will call to me
the way they call
to rabbits

and sun
will move me along
the way it moves
its beetle children

and wind
will blow
my tracks away
with theirs.

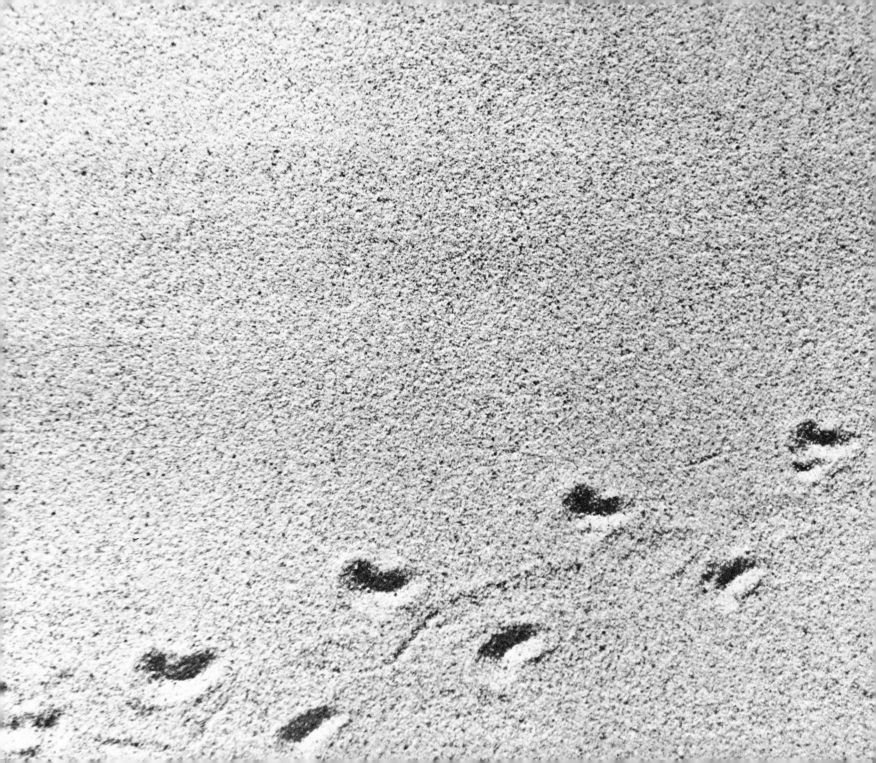